This Preston Pig Story

Belongs To:

. . . .

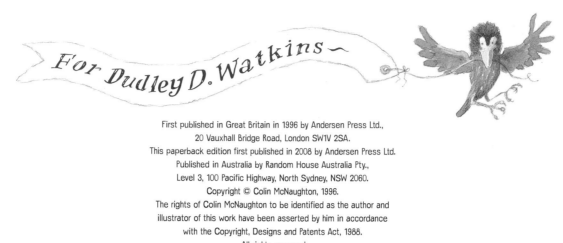

For Dudley D. Watkins

First published in Great Britain in 1996 by Andersen Press Ltd.,
20 Vauxhall Bridge Road, London SW1V 2SA.
This paperback edition first published in 2008 by Andersen Press Ltd.
Published in Australia by Random House Australia Pty.,
Level 3, 100 Pacific Highway, North Sydney, NSW 2060.
Copyright © Colin McNaughton, 1996.
The rights of Colin McNaughton to be identified as the author and
illustrator of this work have been asserted by him in accordance
with the Copyright, Designs and Patents Act, 1988.
Colour separated in Switzerland by Photolitho AG, Zürich.
Printed and bound in Singapore.

10   9   8   7   6   5   4   3   2   1

British Library Cataloguing in Publication Data available.
ISBN 978 1 84270 712 8

Colin McNaughton
Oops!

Andersen Press

It was the same old story.
Mister Wolf was hungry.
Mister Wolf was very hungry
and Mister Wolf had his
eye on Preston Pig.

Mister Wolf was hungry
for three very good reasons:

1. Mister Plimp the shopkeeper
had banned him from his shop
for eating the customers.

2. Mister Plump the park keeper
had banned him from the park
for picnicking on the visitors.

3. Miss Thump the school
teacher had banned him
from the school grounds
for snacking on the students.

"Don't look at me like that,
I'm the Big Bad Wolf!
It's my job to be nasty. These
stories would be
pretty boring if I was
good, wouldn't they?"

Suddenly!

There was a huge crash.
"Oops!" said Preston.

"You clumsy great pudding!"
said Preston's mum. "Get
out from under my feet and
take that basket of food to
your Granny's. She's not well."
"Yes, Mum," said Preston.
"And tell Granny I'll be
over later to chop her some
wood," said Preston's dad.
"Yes, Dad," said Preston.
"And put your coat on,"
said Preston's mum.
"Yes, Mum," said Preston.
"And don't slam the door,"
said Preston's dad.
"The chimney pot is loose…"

"Slam!" went the door.
"Oops!" went Preston.

"Hmm… red hood, basket of food, granny's house? That reminds me of a story, but which one?" said Mister Wolf – just before the chimney pot landed on his head.

Mister Wolf picked himself up
and followed Preston.
"I'll take a short cut through
the woods and get ahead
of him," said Mister Wolf.

Sneaky
short cut

But Mister Wolf did not like
the woods. Woods were full of
nasty, itchy, scratchy, bitey things.

"I wish I could think which story that red hood reminds me of," said Mister Wolf crossly as he pulled thorns out of his bottom.

"I know it isn't *The Three Little Pigs*," said Mister Wolf. "But I do like that story. Especially the bit where the wolf eats the three little pigs and escapes. Well, that's how *my* mum used to tell it!"

Mister Wolf tried some cunning
wolf tricks to catch Preston
but he didn't have much luck.

What a silly place to leave a banana skin. Someone might have slipped on it.

Cunning Wolf Trick No.1
The old 'Banana Skin' ploy.

Cunning Wolf Trick No.2
The old 'Dig-a-Deep-Pit' dodge.

Cunning Wolf Trick No.3
The old 'If-All-Else-Fails-Bash-'em-on-the-Head-with-a-Big-Stick' plan.

Preston reached Granny's house safely. Mister Wolf was fed up. He was hot and sticky, scratched, stung and bitten. "And I still can't remember that rotten story!" said Mister Wolf.

Suddenly!

There was a huge crash.
"Oops!" said Preston.

Mister Wolf sneaked up
to the window and this
is what he heard ...

"What big eyes you've got,
Granny!" said Preston.
"All the better to see you
smash my teapot!" said Granny.

"What big ears you've got,
Granny!" said Preston.
"All the better to hear you
smash my cups!" said Granny.

"What big teeth you've got
Granny!" said Preston.
"All the better to gnash
when you smash my sugar
bowl!" said Granny.

"Hey," cried Mister Wolf, "those are *my* lines! I remember that story now. It's *Little Red Riding Hood.*" Mister Wolf leaped through the window, tied Granny up and stuffed Preston in a sack.

"Now, let me think," said Mister Wolf. "How does that story end?" He was just opening the door when he remembered…

"Oops!"
said Mister Wolf.

Look out!

for the other Preston Pig stories: